Rosie
the Honey Bear
Fairy

With magical love to Lara

Special thanks to
Rachel Elliot

ORCHARD BOOKS
338 Euston Road, London NW1 3BH
Orchard Books Australia
Level 17/207 Kent Street, Sydney, NSW 2000
A Paperback Original

First published in 2013 by Orchard Books

HiT entertainment

A CIP catalogue record for this book is available
from the British Library.

ISBN 978 1 40832 798 2

1 3 5 7 9 10 8 6 4 2

Printed in Great Britain

The paper and board used in this paperback are natural recyclable
products made from wood grown in sustainable forests. The
manufacturing processes conform to the environmental regulations
of the country of origin.

Orchard Books is a division of Hachette Children's Books,
an Hachette UK company

www.hachette.co.uk

Rosie
the Honey Bear
Fairy

by Daisy Meadows

ORCHARD

www.rainbowmagic.co.uk

Wild Woods Nature Reserve

Watering Hole

Pagoda

Jack Frost's Ice Castle

To Jack Frost's Zoo ⟩

Desert Oasis

Jack Frost's Spell

I love animals, yes I do,
I want my very own private zoo!
I'll capture the animals one by one,
With fairy magic to help me on!

A koala, a tiger, an Arctic fox,
I'll keep them in cages with giant locks.
Every kind of animal will be there,
A panda, a meerkat, a honey bear.
The animals will be my property,
I'll be master of a huge menagerie!

Contents

Bees and Butterflies

"I wish it could be summer all year round," cheered Kirsty Tate.

She straightened up from filling her wheelbarrow and smiled at her best friend Rachel Walker. Rachel dropped a small trowel into her own wheelbarrow and smiled back at Kirsty.

"Me too," she said, her cheeks pink from all her hard work. "And I wish we could help out at the nature reserve for longer too. I love the animals so much!"

The girls were spending a week of their summer holidays helping at Wild Woods Nature Reserve as part of a team of junior rangers. Every day, they earned badges for their backpacks by doing special tasks. Becky, the head of the nature reserve, set the tasks. That morning, she had thought of something especially lovely for them to do together.

"I'd like you to plant shrubs along the bank of the stream," she had said. "The shrubs will attract bees and butterflies to the nature reserve. We depend on them to help keep the plants alive."

The girls had filled their wheelbarrows

10

with pots of flowering shrubs, spades, trowels, forks and watering cans.

"We're ready, Becky!" called Kirsty.

"Right," Becky replied with a grin. "Follow me!"

She led them through the woods, and the wheelbarrows bumped over the branches and pinecones on the ground.

When they came out of the woods,
the stream was straight ahead of them.
Beside the clear, sparkling water they
saw a row of little wooden houses on
platforms.

"They look like fairy houses," said
Kirsty excitedly.

She had spoken quietly, but Becky
heard her and laughed.

"Yes," she said. "If
fairies existed, I bet
they'd love to live
in one of these cute
houses! Actually
they're beehives.
The bees will use
the nectar from the
flowers you're planting
to make honey."

Rachel and Kirsty smiled at each
other. They had a secret that bonded
them as best friends forever. They knew
that fairies were real, and they had often
visited Fairyland and shared adventures
with their fairy friends. During one of
their recent visits, the fairies had even
given them the ability to understand
what animals were saying.

Becky led them to a little stone bridge that crossed the stream.

"I'd like you to plant some shrubs on both sides of the stream, close to the bridge," she said. "Do you know how to plant them?"

"Yes," said Rachel. "My mum loves gardening and I've helped her lots of times."

"Great," said Becky. "I'll leave you to it. Call me if you need any help, and have fun!"

As Becky walked away, Rachel pulled on her gardening gloves and Kirsty looked around the area.

"Let's start on this side of the bridge," Kirsty suggested.

"Yes, and I think I'll plant a pink shrub first," said Rachel. "What about you?"

"Blue!" said Kirsty, picking a pretty little plant out of her wheelbarrow. "Let's get digging!"

They picked up their spades and started to dig two holes. After a short while, a group of colourful butterflies fluttered towards them. As they hovered over the holes, the girls heard a babble of tiny, curious voices.

"What are they doing?"

"Why is she opening the ground up?"

"What's going on?"

Rachel laughed and paused, resting one foot on the shoulder of her spade.

"Hello, butterflies," she said. "We're planting some flowering shrubs so that you'll want to come back here."

"That's wonderful!" twittered the butterflies all together. "Thank you! Thank you!"

Suddenly, among the wafting wings of the butterflies, Kirsty spotted a flash of blue glinting in the sunlight.

"Oh, is that a fairy?" she asked in excitement.

Rachel whipped her head around to look where Kirsty was pointing. She screwed up her eyes against the bright sunlight, and then shook her head.

"It's a big blue dragonfly," she said. "But even so, I have a funny feeling…"

"Me too," said Kirsty. "Like there's magic nearby!"

Magical Pooh Sticks

Rachel and Kirsty kept digging, watched closely by the butterflies. They knew that if there was magic around, it would find them when the time was right.

As they worked, the girls thought about the busy week they were having. As well as helping at Wild Woods Nature Reserve, they were also helping the

Baby Animal Rescue Fairies. Animals all
around the world needed to be protected
from Jack Frost and his pesky goblins.

On their first day at the human
nature reserve, Rachel and Kirsty had
met Bertram, the frog footman from
Fairyland, who was visiting relatives
at the pond. He had whisked the girls
away to the nature reserve in Fairyland.
There they had spent time with the Baby
Animal Rescue Fairies, who looked after
animals in both Fairyland and in the
human world. But Jack Frost and his
goblins were up to mischief. Jack had
decided that he liked animals so much,
he wanted to collect one of each kind for
his own private zoo – by any means!

Kirsty and Rachel tried to tell Jack
Frost that animals weren't like collectable

toys. They needed
lots of care! But
he sneered at
them and stole
the Baby Animal
Rescue Fairies'
magical key
rings, which helped them to protect the
animals. He gave the magical key rings
to his goblins and ordered them to get
some animals from the human world for
his zoo. All animals were now in danger!

The seven fairies had given Kirsty and
Rachel the power to talk to animals
when they offered to protect them. Five
baby animals had already been saved
from Jack Frost. Would they need to
help the Baby Animal Rescue Fairies
save some more animals today?

As they planted the shrubs, the girls wondered excitedly about the adventures they might have. The butterflies fluttered nearer and nearer.

"It's going to be so lovely to have some beautiful plants to visit round here," said a large red admiral, very close to Kirsty's ear.

"Oh, your wings are tickling my cheek!" Kirsty giggled.

"I do apologise," said the butterfly, moving away at once. "We're very excited to see all the changes that have been going on."

"Me too," added the blue dragonfly.

"I've been flying all over the nature reserve. You junior rangers are doing a grand job. Thank you!"

"Can you hear something buzzing?" asked Kirsty as she took her shrub out of its pot.

"It's the bees!" the butterflies began to twitter among themselves. "Now we'll have some fun!"

Kirsty felt a little bit nervous when a dark cloud of bees swarmed around them, but they soon put her at ease.

"New flowers?"

"For us?"

"Wonderful!"

"We're buzzing with excitement!"

The insects swooped over the water and turned somersaults in the air as the girls planted shrub after shrub in the ground.

"I'm going to make a start on the other side of the stream," said Kirsty at last.

Rachel nodded, and Kirsty picked up a
pot and started to walk over the bridge.
Halfway across, she paused and bent
down to pick up a twig and dropped
it into the gurgling stream. Then she
rushed to the other side to watch it float
out from under the bridge.

"Let's play Pooh Sticks!" said Rachel,
who had been watching her best friend.

The girls pulled off their gloves and
each chose a twig. They dropped them
into the water and then hung over the
side of the bridge to see who would win.
The insects watched and cheered as
Kirsty's twig edged into the lead. Then,
suddenly, Rachel spotted something
strange in the water.

"Look at that leaf," she said. "Does it look *different* to you?"

She pointed to a small leaf that was floating downstream towards the bridge. It was glowing!

The bees whizzed down to the leaf, and then zoomed back to the girls in a spiralling swarm.

"It's not a leaf!" they buzzed. "It's Rosie the Honey Bear Fairy!"

Surprise in a Hive

The girls hung over the side of the bridge and watched Rosie fly up to them. She perched on the stone bridge and gave Rachel and Kirsty a big smile. She was wearing a sparkly blue top, light blue jeans, and her honey-blonde hair was tousled.

"It looks like you're having fun!" she said. "I'm sorry, but I'm here to drag

you away from your game. A baby bear
is missing, and I really need your help to
find him. Will you come with me?"

"Of course we'll come," said Rachel
and Kirsty at once.

Rosie winked and waved her wand in
a circle above her head, making a hoop
of sparkling fairy dust. It grew wider and
wider, until it surrounded the girls and
whisked them away in a trice.

They blinked, and found themselves
looking down over a lush wooded valley.
There were tall trees all around them,
and the leaves were rustling in the gentle
breeze. The ground was soft with layers
of mulched leaves and twigs.

"Hello, Mama Bear," said Rosie in a
gentle voice.

The girls looked around and saw an

enormous brown bear sitting on a rock
in a clearing. She was holding a dripping
honeycomb in her paw, but she wasn't
eating it. They stepped closer and saw
that tears were trickling down her
furry cheeks.

"What's the matter?" asked Kirsty,
putting her hand on the bear's furry paw.
"Can we help you?"

"It's my baby, Billy," said Mama Bear with a little sob. "He's gone missing!"

The girls gave a suspicious glance.

"I'm sure the goblins are behind this," Rachel said.

"If they are, I promise we'll stop them," Kirsty told Mama Bear. "We'll find your little Billy and bring him home safe and sound."

Just then, a bee buzzed out from behind Mama Bear's head.

"Billy's missing?" it exclaimed, sounding upset. "He's my friend! How can I help?"

"Have you seen anything unusual in the valley?" Kirsty asked. "Like strange green creatures?"

"The Queen Bee might know something," said the little bee. "If you follow me, I'll take you to her straight away!"

Rachel and Kirsty turned to Rosie. If they were going to visit the Queen Bee, they were going to have to be fairy-sized. With a flick of Rosie's wand, the girls were transformed into fairies. Now that they were tiny, they could see the kind expression on the bee's furry face.

33

His wings made a loud, whirring sound, and created a breeze that fanned the girls' faces. He gave them a little smile.

"Follow me," he said. "I'll take you to the Queen Bee."

"We'll be back as soon as we can, Mama Bear," said Rosie.

They waved to the sad-faced bear, and then followed the little bee up to the top of a tree, where his hive was nestled among green leaves.

34

It looked like a small
city towering
above them.

The bee
led them to
the entrance,
where two
guard bees were
hovering.

"These are my
guests," said the bee. "They want to visit
the Queen Bee."

"Welcome to our hive," said the
guard bees.

The girls followed their friend into
the straw-coloured lower chamber. The
walls were full of honeycomb cells. The
Queen Bee was sitting on her throne
in the centre of the chamber. She was

surrounded by drone bees, who were combing her fur and polishing her wings.

Rachel and Kirsty gasped. They recognised that royal fuzzy face!

"It's Queenie!" said Rachel, flitting forward to greet their old friend.

The last time they had seen Queenie, she was living with the Rainbow Fairies in the pot-at-the-end-of-the-rainbow.

"Rachel! Kirsty!" Queenie exclaimed. "How lovely to see you!"

"You too," said Kirsty. "But we thought you were living with the Rainbow Fairies."

"I had a lovely time there," said Queenie, "but I missed the other bees. So now I'm the queen of this hive. Come, dear girls, sit yourselves down, have some nectar and tell me what brings you here."

Noisy Hikers

The drone bees brought acorn cups full
of delicious nectar. Rachel and Kirsty
sipped their drinks and talked with
Queenie about their adventures with the
Rainbow Fairies. Then they told her
about Billy the little bear going missing.

"I'm very sorry to hear that," said
Queenie. "Billy is very sweet and all the
bees love him."

"Excuse me, Your Majesty," said one of the drone bees. "The park ranger knows everything that happens in the valley. Perhaps he's seen something unusual that will help these fairies find little Billy?"

"Excellent idea," said Queenie.

The girls finished their drinks and stood up. Queenie nodded to two of her drone bees, and they buzzed forward carrying a scrumptious-looking piece of honeycomb.

"Share that with Billy when you find him," said Queenie. "It's been lovely to see you again, girls."

She commanded a swarm of bees to
lead them to the park ranger. Rosie,
Kirsty and Rachel zoomed along behind
the bees as they weaved among the trees.

At last they heard the sound of a man
whistling up ahead.

"That's the park ranger!" said their bee
friends. "Good luck!"

As the bees buzzed away, Kirsty and
Rachel fluttered down and landed
behind a bush. Hovering above them,
Rosie waved her wand and turned them
back into humans.

"Right," said Rachel. "Let's find out what that park ranger knows."

She tucked the honeycomb into her backpack and Rosie jumped in too, glad to rest her wings. They tramped through the wood, following the sound of the whistling. The park ranger was standing on a grassy mound overlooking the wooded valley.

"Excuse me?" Kirsty called out.

The park ranger whirled around. He had a friendly tanned face and spiky brown hair.

"Hello!" he said. "What can I do for you?"

"We were just wondering if you had seen anything unusual in the valley today?" Kirsty asked. "We're…er… looking for someone."

The park ranger nodded.

"There was a group of noisy hikers here earlier," he said. "I had to warn them to be quiet or they would scare the wildlife."

Rachel squeezed Kirsty's hand.

"What did they look like?" she asked.

"They looked a bit silly to be honest," the park ranger said with a chuckle. "They were wearing bright green hiking gear with the biggest hiking boots I've ever seen, and one of them had a backpack filled to the brim. Friends of yours, are they?"

"Not exactly," said Kirsty, gritting her teeth.

"Do you know where they went?" Rachel asked.

The park ranger pointed to a curving path that led downwards through the woods.

"That leads to the river at the bottom of the valley," he said. "That's where they were heading. You might still catch them, if you're quick."

"Thank you!" said Rachel. "Come on,

44

Kirsty. Let's go!"

She set off down the path, with Kirsty close behind her. They broke into a jog, and Rosie clung on tight to the inside of Rachel's backpack. It was hard to run in the hot midday sun, but they had to stop the goblins.

With a final curve, the path opened out
on the side of a large, meandering river.
Rachel held out her arm to stop Kirsty.

"Look, there they are!" she said.

There were three goblins on the other
side of the river, pushing each other and
squabbling. On the ground between
them was a small raft.

"There's a bridge!" said Kirsty, pointing downstream. "Come on!"

The girls ran down the riverbank and raced over the humpback bridge to the opposite bank. The goblins turned and scowled at them.

"What are you doing here?"

"Pesky humans!"

"Leave us alone!"

There was no sign of Billy. Rachel put her hands on her hips.

"What have you done with the bear cub, goblins?" she asked.

The goblins glanced at each other.

"Don't know what you're talking about," said the first goblin, going very red in the face.

"You're fibbing," Kirsty stated, folding her arms across her chest.

"Prove it!" said the second goblin.

The third goblin stuck out his very long tongue and blew a loud raspberry.

"Billy *must* be here somewhere," said Rachel.

"And my magical key ring, too," Rosie added, sticking her head out of Rachel's backpack.

"But *where*?" asked Kirsty.

Branching Out!

Just then, one of the goblins started to push the raft into the water, turning his back to the girls. Now they could see the enormous green backpack that the park ranger had mentioned. As he had said, it was packed to the brim.

"What could the goblins need that would fill such a big bag?" Rachel wondered aloud.

Suddenly, the backpack seemed to wriggle.

"It moved!" cried Rosie. "Girls, the backpack moved!"

"I saw it too," said Kirsty.

As they watched, a furry little snout poked out of the top of the backpack. It was followed by a pair of shining brown eyes and two fuzzy ears.

"It's Billy!" exclaimed Rosie.

"Look, he's got your magical key ring," Rachel added with a smile.

Billy had pushed one paw out of the bag, and he was holding on tight to a fluffy key ring in the shape of a bear.

The girls dashed forwards to try to stop the goblins getting away. But two of them were already on board. As Rachel and Kirsty reached the water's edge, the third jumped onto the raft too. It slid out of reach, and the goblins laughed and jeered as they floated away.

With one swift wave of Rosie's wand, Rachel and Kirsty were fairies again.

"Let's fly among the trees on the riverbank," Rosie suggested. "Let them think they've left us behind."

The girls zoomed along, darting between the trees and keeping level with the little raft. It was bobbing up and down on the fast-flowing water.

Suddenly Rachel gave a cry.

"Billy's climbing out of the backpack!" she exclaimed.

The goblins hadn't noticed that Billy was free. Just then, Rachel saw a fallen branch jutting out of the water.

"Oh no!" she cried. "The raft's heading straight towards that branch!"

The raft wobbled and then veered around the branch. The girls let out sighs of relief.

"That gives me an idea," said Kirsty. "Remember that humpback bridge further downstream? We need to get there before the raft!"

Rachel, Kirsty and Rosie zoomed to the bridge as fast as they could. As they flew, Kirsty explained her plan.

"We just have to hope that Billy Bear really loves honey!" she said with a smile.

When they reached the bridge, Rosie turned the girls into humans again. Then she used her magic to bring the fallen branch from the river to the bridge. Rachel dug into her backpack and pulled out the honeycomb that Queenie had given them earlier.

"Rub the honey all over the branch," said Kirsty. "Quickly!"

Rachel covered the branch in honey, and then the girls dangled it over the edge of the bridge, holding on to the top end.

"I hope Billy Bear sees it!" said Kirsty.

"Please let him make a grab for the honey!" Rachel added.

Their plan was ready – all it needed was for Billy to play his part!

Just then, the goblin raft floated around the bend in the river. It was bobbing along with Billy on the back, but the magical key ring was no longer dangling from his paw.

"Where's my magical key ring gone?" asked Rosie.

There was no time to find out the answer – the raft was about to pass under the bridge!

Billy noticed the
honey dripping
from the branch,
and reached up
to it. His long
tongue began to
lick the honey,
and he started to
climb the log.

"Yes, Billy!"
called Rachel.
"Good bear! Keep coming!"
She and Kirsty held on tight to the
branch, taking the bear's weight. Below,
the goblins squawked in dismay and
clutched at the stone sides of the bridge,
trying to slow the raft down.

"No, Billy!" shouted the goblin with
the backpack. "Bad bear! Come back!"

"Billy!" called another of the goblins. "Look here, Billy!"

The goblin held up the magical key ring, which he knew would lure the cub back. Billy looked down and then started to slide back down the branch.

"No, come back!" Kirsty cried. "Billy!"

The little bear reached out one paw to get the key ring. The goblin jerked his hand backwards, and sent the magical key ring flying into the river!

Bees, Bears and Badges

Rosie swooped down after the key ring and the goblin jumped into the water with a loud bellyflop. Rachel and Kirsty watched Rosie dive into the river, but they couldn't do anything to help. Billy was clambering up the honey-covered branch again, and the girls needed all their strength to hold on to it.

It seemed to take forever before Billy's little paws were in reach, but at last Rachel was able to grasp them and pull him up to safety. The girls gave him a big cuddle.

"We're going to take you home to your mama," Kirsty told him.

"What about Rosie?" asked Rachel, holding Billy while he finished the honey.

At that moment, Rosie flew up from the other side of the bridge. She shook off sparkling drops of river water and gave a whoop of triumph.

"I got it!" she cried happily.

Rachel and Kirsty gave broad smiles when they saw that she was holding her magical key ring. It had magically shrunk to fairy-size, and it was back where it belonged at last.

"We did it!" said Rosie, hovering beside the girls and Billy.

"What about the goblins?" Rachel asked.

They all leaned over the bridge and
saw the dripping wet goblin being hauled
back onto the raft.

"You two are going to be in big
trouble with Jack Frost when we get
back without the bear cub," he snarled
at the other goblins.

"It was *you* who dropped the stupid
key ring!" snapped the second goblin.

"We're *all* going to be locked up in the
dungeon!" wailed the third goblin.

The raft floated away down the river, and the sound of the goblins' bickering travelled across the water. The girls could hear it even after the raft disappeared from sight.

"Come on," said Rosie. "Let's get this little cub back to his mama."

The girls hiked back the way they had come, up the winding path that led out of the valley. Rachel and Kirsty took turns carrying Billy, and Rosie dangled her key ring in front of him to keep him happy.

They went back through the woods
and at last they reached the clearing
where Mama Bear was still sitting on
the rock.

When she saw her baby, Mama
Bear's eyes filled with happy tears. She
lumbered over to him, scooped him into
her arms and hugged him tightly.

"I've missed you, little one," she
whispered in an amazingly gentle voice.

Billy gave her a snuffly kiss, and she

pressed a honeycomb treat into his paw.
Then she looked up at the girls.

"How can I ever thank you?" she
asked.

"We're just glad that Billy's back
where he belongs," said Rachel.

The cub held out his arms to her, and
she let him give her a little bear hug.
Kirsty got a hug too,
and they were
about to say
goodbye when
there was a
loud buzzing
noise. It was
a huge swarm
of bees, and
between them
they were carrying

two little walnut shells filled with honey.

One bee buzzed to the front of the
swarm and the girls saw that it was the
one they had met here earlier.

"Our beloved queen has sent you this
gift," he said. "To thank you for finding
our friend Billy, please accept this honey.
It's some of our very best!"

"Thank you very much," said Rachel,
taking one of the shells.

"Please give Queenie our love," Kirsty

added, taking the other shell.

While the bees gave them three cheers, Rosie waved her wand and transported them back to Wild Woods. Rachel let out a happy sigh and gazed around. Then her eyes fell on her wheelbarrow.

"Oh my goodness!" she exclaimed. "We haven't finished planting the shrubs yet."

"Let's get to work then," said Kirsty.

The bees and butterflies were still
flitting around the colourful flowers,
and they had been joined by several
more beautiful blue dragonflies. Rosie
went to join them, and had fun playing
while Rachel and Kirsty finished planting
their shrubs.

At last the work was done. The girls
filled their watering cans from the clear
stream and watered each plant. Then
they sat down on the bank and rested.

"It's beautiful here," said Rosie,
coming to land on Rachel's knee.

"It reminds me of the nature reserve in
Fairyland. And
these flowers
smell wonderful."

"The honey
we make from
the nectar will be
absolutely delicious,"
said a bee as he circled
around Kirsty's head. "I can't wait!"

"Ooh, someone's coming!" said a
little cabbage-white butterfly in a panic.
"Hide, Rosie!"

With a goodbye
wave, Rosie
flew onto a blue
flower and hid
among the petals.
Then the girls saw
Becky striding towards
them from the woods. She looked at the
planting they had done and then smiled.

"Excellent work, both of you," she
said. "These look perfect. You've
definitely earned your badges today."

From one of the big pockets in her
cargo shorts, she drew out two flower-
shaped badges. As she handed them to
Rachel and Kirsty, a bee zoomed under
her nose.

"The flowers are already attracting lots
of insects," she said.

"And a fairy too," said Rachel in a tiny whisper.

She and Kirsty looked over at the blue flower where Rosie was hiding and squeezed one another's hand. They had really enjoyed their adventure with the Honey Bear Fairy. But there was still one magical key ring to find. They hoped that they would meet Anna the Arctic Fox Fairy tomorrow!

Now it's time for Kirsty and Rachel to help...

Anna the Arctic Fox Fairy

Read on for a sneak peek...

"Isn't it a beautiful evening?" Rachel Walker remarked to her best friend, Kirsty Tate, glancing up at the night sky strewn with tiny, glittering stars. The evening air was warm and still, and above the trees the moon shone with a pale, silvery light.

"It's a lovely way to end our week at Wild Woods," Kirsty agreed. The girls had volunteered to spend part of their summer holidays at the nature reserve near Kirsty's home, learning how to be junior rangers. Now it was their last day, and all the volunteers were waiting outside the wildlife centre for Becky, the manager of Wild Woods, to join them for a special evening.

"It's really kind of Becky to take us on a night-time walk," Rachel said. "I hope we see lots of different animals."

"Becky said it was a special treat because we'd all worked so hard," Kirsty reminded her. "Although we *do* have our badges as well!"

Both girls stared proudly at the pockets of their backpacks which were covered with badges. Every time they'd completed their tasks successfully, Becky had given them a badge, and the girls had six so far.

Read **Anna the Arctic Fox Fairy** to find out what adventures are in store for Kirsty and Rachel!

Meet the
Baby Animal Rescue
Fairies

The Baby Animal Rescue Fairies have lost all their magical
items. But luckily, Kirsty and Rachel are there to
save the day and make sure all baby animals
in the world are safe and sound.

www.rainbowmagicbooks.co.uk

Look out for the next sparkly
Rainbow Magic Special!

Robyn the Christmas Party Fairy

Rachel and Kirsty are helping to organise a big Christmas party.
But Jack Frost has stolen Robyn the Christmas Party Fairy's
magical objects! The girls must help Robyn,
before the spirit of Christmas is lost forever...

Out now!

RAINBOW magic

Meet the fairies, play games
and get sneak peeks at
the latest books!

www.rainbowmagicbooks.co.uk

There's fairy fun for everyone on
our wonderful website.
You'll find great activities, competitions, stories and
fairy profiles, and also a special newsletter.

Get 30% off all Rainbow Magic books at
www.rainbowmagicbooks.co.uk

Enter the code RAINBOW at the checkout.
Offer ends 31 December 2013.

Offer valid in United Kingdom and Republic of Ireland only.

...mpetition!

...e Baby Animal Rescue Fairies have created
a special competition just for you!
In the back of each book in the series there will be
a question for you to answer.
Once you have collected all the books and all
seven answers, go online and enter the competition!

We will put all the correct entries into a draw and select
a winner to receive a special Rainbow Magic Goody Bag,
featuring lots of treats for you and your fairy friends.
The winner will also star in a new Rainbow Magic story!

What colour hair does Esme the Ice Cream Fairy have?

_ _ _ _ _

Enter online now at www.rainbowmagicbooks.co.uk

No purchase required. Only one entry per child.
Two prize draws will take place on 1st April 2014 and 2nd July 2014. Alternatively readers can
send the answer on a postcard to: Rainbow Magic, Baby Animal Rescue Fairies Competition,
Orchard Books, 338 Euston Road, London, NW1 3BH. Australian readers can write to:
Rainbow Magic, Baby Animal Rescue Fairies Competition, Hachette Children's Books,
level 17/207 Kent St, Sydney, NSW 2000. E-mail: childrens.books@hachette.com.au.
New Zealand readers should write to:
Rainbow Magic, Baby Animal Rescue Fairies Competition,
4 Whetu Place, Mairangi Bay, Auckland, NZ

Meet the
Rainbow Fairies

Ruby
the Red
Fairy

Amber
the Orange
Fairy

Saffron
the Yellow
Fairy

Fern
the Green
Fairy

Sky
the Blue
Fairy

Izzy
the Indigo
Fairy

Heather
the Violet
Fairy

**Also available
as an ebook**

Collect the seven original Rainbow Fairies
to find out how the adventure began!

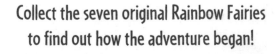

www.rainbowmagicbooks.co.uk